LISA VAN DER WIELEN

Ripples

RIPPLES

Ripples

For all those seeking the truth, may the ripples

reach the shore.

By

Lisa Van Der Wielen

RIPPLES

First Printed 2026

Copyright © Lisa Van Der Wielen

The moral right of the author has been asserted.

ISBN: 9781763534490 (Paperback)
ISBN: 9781764477000 (Hardback)

Cover and text design by Lisa Van Der Wielen

Set in Times New Roman

www.lisavanderwielen.com

Contents

RIPPLES

Chapter 1

Voices

Anna couldn't sleep. Faint sparkles of light from the streetlamps were peeping through the gaps in the blinds, which moved gently to the soft sea breeze that blew through the open window. At her feet, the dog stretched out to catch any cool air wafting through the room. Anna tried to close her eyes to rest but it was too hard. It was summer, and the warmth in the room made it difficult to breathe, let alone sleep.

She decided to get up for a glass of cold water. As she tip-toed quietly through the kitchen she heard a noise coming from the back of the house. Perhaps, she told herself, it was the neighbour's cat trying to get through the doggy door once again to steal food. As she crept closer to the back of the house, she heard a voice and some giggling. Laughter is not something Anna had heard in her household for a very long time. Especially since her mother had disappeared, presumed dead at sea.

Anna's home was usually a very quiet place - so quiet you could hear the waves crashing on the shoreline at night. As she peered through the opening in the curtains out into the back yard, a strange feeling swept over her. *Who was it? Who was standing there in her yard creating a silhouette in the moonlight?* Anna stood motionless, holding the edge of the curtain in her hand as she tried to work out the details of the figure standing in her garden.

Her mind raced. *Should I scream? Should I turn the light on? Should I call for Dad, or the police?* As much as she was scared, Anna was also very calm; it was almost as if she knew this person, whoever it was, was not there to harm her. As she stood in the dark room peering out, she heard Scruffy run through the doggy door and into the backyard, giving a little bark as he disappeared into the darkness.

"Scruff, what are you barking at?" she heard her father say jovially, followed by a laugh – but not her dad's laugh. This was a woman's laugh.

"Hello, Scruff," said the woman chirpily. Anna had heard that voice before, it sounded familiar. While she couldn't quite make out the identity of the woman standing in her backyard, Anna did notice her dad stroke her as if she were made of gold. Her stomach felt like a sinking ship. *Who is this woman my dad is chatting with so affectionately late at night in our backyard?*

Anna was so engrossed she didn't even notice the glass of water slipping from her hand. BANG! CRASH! The glass smashed into pieces, spreading shards of glass everywhere.

Anna's father ran inside. "Are you okay? What happened?" He sounded concerned.

"Who is that outside? Who are you talking to?" Anna questioned. "I heard a voice and Scruff was barking."

Anna's father went silent for a moment, as if he were contemplating what to reply. Finally he spoke. "I wasn't talking to anyone Anna, no one was outside with me," he said an attempt at breeziness. "I was just sitting outside having some time to myself when Scruff came outside barking. You must be imagining things. Maybe you need to see your counsellor more; you've been imagining a lot of things lately. Grief can do that to people. It's important you talk to someone."

Anna didn't know how to respond. She knew she wasn't going crazy; she knew what she saw and heard but didn't have the energy to debate her father's gaslighting. She quietly began sweeping up the broken glass from the floor, holding Scruffy under one arm. Then she poured another glass of water and retreated to her bedroom as quicky as she could. Scruff followed her to the bedroom as if he were her shadow, making himself comfortable again at the foot of the bed. Anna heard her father turn the lights off in the kitchen before taking himself off to bed without saying another word.

Since she lost her mother, Anna's relationship with her father, Richard, had become strained and their communication was minimal. Anna couldn't help but feel her father was hiding something. He had always had a suave persona, which most people put down to his field of work as a surgeon, but Anna would describe him as emotionless. She didn't trust him; in fact, she didn't trust many people and always kept to herself. Some days, the grief from the loss of her mother consumed her and going to school was just too difficult. On the days she had the energy to attend, she would sit at the back of the classroom, or on a bench away from others, so she could just watch people and the world go by. The school had been very understanding of the circumstances and allowed her to do most of her studies at home for her final year. Her final exams were approaching, and Anna was unsure what she wanted to do when she left school. She felt lost in a big world, looking for answers.

As Anna lay in bed waiting for a gasp of breeze to cool down the room, she could not stop thinking about the voice of the woman she had heard in her backyard. There was a slight crackle sound to her laugh that seemed familiar, and the sound of that giggle kept repeating itself in Anna's head. Her brain wouldn't stop thinking. She knew she wasn't imagining what she saw and heard - even Scruffy had barked at the woman. Feeling determined to find out the truth about the woman in her backyard, Anna eventually fell asleep to the sound of the soft sea breeze drifting through her room.

Chapter 2

Capsized

Anna's mother Kate disappeared one year ago, when Anna was just sixteen. Her parents' yacht had capsized in croc-infested waters, and her mother was declared dead at sea. Anna's parents often sailed around the islands of North Queensland in their large white yacht. Sometimes Anna would go with them but on this occasion she wasn't included, so she stayed with her Aunt Jane, who lived two streets away. Anna took Scruff with her, and she was able to come back to the house whenever she liked. Aunt Jane was just like Anna's mum Kate. Both of them were kind souls, always wanting to help people and putting others first. They were creative people in touch with nature. Anna was lucky to have an aunty looking out for her when her mum disappeared, although Jane was grieving just as much as Anna, and she had children of her own to look after. So as the time grew following Kate's disappearance, so did the distance between Anna and her aunt. Life became difficult for both of them and survival mode set in. Anna was starting to wonder if Jane distanced herself from her for a reason; she had never been fond of Anna's father Richard. Anna felt very alone at times, almost as if her father wanted it that way.

Anna's mum Kate had loved nature, especially the sea. She was a famous landscape photographer in Queensland and her prints sold all around the world. It was why they lived in the coastal town of Sunrise Beach. Kate would often sit with Anna on the beach and encourage her to get in tune with nature by listening to the sounds of the ocean and watching the glistening ripples of water. There was one particular day Anna had spent with her mum at the beach taking photos at sunrise, shortly before Kate went missing, that Anna remembered distinctly. Her mother's words that day still echoed in Anna's head, as if she was trying to tell Anna something, while also protecting her from the truth.

"See the ripples of water? They travel across the vast expanses of the open ocean, but eventually all waves must reach the shore. Lies, just like ripples, must travel before reaching the shore, but eventually they reveal themselves, somewhere."

Anna still didn't understand what her mother meant, but she was determined to find out. *What lies was she referring to? Was she protecting her while also giving her a hint about something going on?*

Anna's parents had only been away on their yacht for a few days when the terrible news came in that their boat had capsized in the waters of the Coral Sea. Anna had been eating dinner at the time with Aunt Jane and her cousins, who were laughing at a cartoon on the television. It was the first time Anna had felt like she was part of a proper family with siblings. Jane's mobile phone had rung, and Anna watched the concern on her face as she spoke to the person on the other end of the phone. As she hung up the phone, the tears began rolling down her face.

"What's wrong?" Anna asked.

"It's your parents," said Aunt Jane. "Their boat has capsized, and Richard and Kate are missing. The search party is looking for them now and they will keep us updated with any news. I am so sorry Anna. But it is going to be okay. Your mum is a good swimmer; I am sure they will find your parents soon and everything will be okay." Aunt Jane was trying to be strong and reassuring. "The search party won't give up until they find them."

Anna felt her stomach sink and an overwhelming feeling of anxiety sweep over her. She had so many questions.

"Where did the boat capsize? Are they far out to sea? Can we go there now?" she pleaded.

"They didn't tell me the exact location, only that the boat has capsized in the Coral Sea, east of Marion Reef," Jane replied. "We can't just go there, it's nine hundred kilometres to Mackay, where the search party is based."

"I can drive there myself, I can't sit around doing nothing, I need to go and help!" Anna's voice raised with her anxiety.

"Anna, you can't drive there yourself, you only have your learner's licence and it's a ten-hour drive. Let's just wait for more news and we will take it from there. It is going to be okay," Jane reassured Anna.

The evening passed painfully for Anna, the seconds slowly turning to minutes and the minutes into hours. The waiting seemed to take forever. Finally, at two twenty-two in the morning, the phone rang.

"Hello, have you found them?" Jane nervously questioned.

"Jane, it's me, Richard. I have just been rescued and I'm here with the Mackay Marine Rescue.

I'm okay, but the search team are still out looking for Kate."

"What have you done with her, Richard? What happened? You know those waters are infested with crocodiles, not to mention sharks and those lethal jellyfish. How did you let this happen?" Jane spoke with anger in her voice.

Questions also started forming in Anna's head. *Why was Dad found and not Mum? Why had Aunt Jane never liked my father? Why did my father not even ask to speak to me or check if I was doing okay?*

As she hung up the phone, Jane began to sob loudly. "I am so sorry Anna, I can't believe this is happening. I think we best try and get some sleep and hopefully we'll receive some good news in the morning."

Anna was speechless. She didn't know what to say, she didn't know what to do. It was like her body was frozen, but her mind was racing. She wanted to feel positive, but she couldn't help but feel her mum was gone. Anna lay on the couch looking out at the full, round moon lighting up the sky, tears rolling down her cheeks. *What if I never see my mother again? What if she was trying to tell me something last week in her cryptic ripples message?*

There was no way Anna was going to fall asleep knowing her mother was lost at sea - or even worse, under the sea. Anna wasn't religious, but this night she prayed and prayed for her mother to be okay. As the sun started to peak over the ocean, Anna woke her aunt, pleading her to drive to Mackay to help search for her mother. One of her cousins turned on the television, and as he waited for his cartoon show to begin, Anna heard the newsreader cut in:

"A yacht belonging to a Queensland couple has capsized in the Coral Sea. Photographer Kate Mears is yet to be found, with search parties still looking for her."

Anna's heart sank and tears began rolling down her cheeks once again. She couldn't help but feel her mother was already gone, even though she was holding onto hope as best she could. The hours of waiting turned into days, and Anna's body felt numb from pain and despair. She couldn't eat, she could barely function and going to school for her final year eleven exams wasn't an option. Facing people and answering all their questions was not something Anna was looking forward to. News travelled fast, and cooked meals from kindly locals were already being placed at the front door. Four days into the search, the Mackay Marine Rescue called off the search for Kate Mears, declaring her likely dead at sea. However, as Anna learned, a person can only be declared 'presumed dead' after they have been missing for seven years. That is a long time for someone to finally be declared dead, Anna thought. A very long time of waiting and wondering without closure.

One week later, an honest Mackay local handed in some pieces of gold jewellery found washed up on Harbour Beach in a shoe. There was a wedding ring engraved with the initials 'RM' and a bracelet with a gold locket engraved with the word 'Forever'. The Mackay police immediately suspected they were linked to the disappearance of Kate Mears, and it was later confirmed that the shoe, ring and bracelet were indeed Kate's, and the police kept them for evidence. Even though these items suggested Kate was likely no longer alive, Anna wanted answers as to how and why they were washed up ashore in her shoe. Her father said she was wearing them when the boat capsized.

Anna knew she wouldn't get any answers from her father. Every question she had ever asked him about the incident since he returned was answered with the disingenuous approach of a politician. Anna didn't trust her father. She hardly knew him; he was always working at the hospital or sailing on his yacht or attending medical board meetings out of town. Anna didn't have many friends; she wouldn't allow herself to get too close to others, preferring to spend most of her time alone or with her mother, which is why her mother's disappearance had hit Anna like a tidal wave. Anna now felt like she had no one. Her Aunt Jane was very supportive, but she had her family to deal with, and she was dealing with her own grief. In the aftermath of the tragedy, Anna had hardly slept. Her father had suggested medication to help her, but Anna wouldn't have a bar of it.

Chapter 3

Sara

The morning sun beamed through small gaps in the blinds. Anna woke to find Scruffy still sleeping at her feet. Immediately, thoughts of what had happened the night before started to creep into Anna's mind. She was determined to find out who it was in her backyard last night. She was still looking for answers to her mothers' disappearance, but every time she brought up the incident to her father, he didn't want to talk about it, wanting to focus on the future and positivity. It was difficult for Anna to grieve for her mother's disappearance, not knowing what her fate was that day, almost one year ago. She continued to hold onto a small amount of hope that her favourite person was still alive out there somewhere, but she couldn't help but feel, deep down, that she was gone. Anna knew that if her mother were alive, there is no way she would leave Anna alone, thinking she was gone.

Anna carefully hopped out of bed, trying to avoid disturbing Scruffy. As she made her way to the bathroom, a sunset orange scarf fell down from the hat rack in the hallway. Anna picked it up. It was so soft, made from pure Chinese silk. It was Kate's scarf, a gift from her friend Sara when they had travelled together many years ago. It made Anna think of Sara. *Maybe she knows something about Mum's disappearance, and she is the person I need to speak to for answers.* Anna placed the delicate scarf back onto the rack and headed to the bathroom. Suddenly she had plans for the day - she was going to visit Sara.

Anna remembered going to Sara's house with her mother when she was younger, but it had been many years since she had seen her. The only hope Anna had was to try and remember where she lived. As Anna grabbed her car keys, Scruffy wagged his tail at the front door.

"Sorry Scruff, not today, you will have to stay home," said Anna as she left the house.

Anna turned on the engine to her car and looked into the rear vision mirror, only to see her father returning from his morning run.

"Where are you off to?" he asked.

Anna wound down her car window. She didn't like lying, but didn't want to let her dad know she was looking for answers to her mother's disappearance.

"I'm just off to a friend's place to do some study," she replied, as she reversed out of the driveway in her little white car displaying 'P' plates.

Anna recalled Sara didn't live far away, only ten minutes down the coast at Peregian Beach. Driving through the once-familiar streets, it was not like she remembered. New apartment blocks and units had been built, and Anna found it hard to find her bearings. After driving through the streets for some time she eventually found the place she was looking for. She remembered the large wall out the front and the white tin roof, which now sported large solar panels. It seemed more modern looking than she remembered, but she was sure she had the right location. As she pulled into the driveway, nerves began to wash over her. *What will Sara think about her arriving unannounced? What was she thinking, just driving straight over to her house?*

Anna sat in the car for a moment before she worked up the courage to get out and walk to the front door. She knocked three times. Within moments, a tall young man opened the door.

"Hello," he said.

He had tanned skin with scruffy sun-bleached hair and a lovely smile. At first, Anna thought that she had the wrong house, but then she remembered Sara had a son about a year older than her. She hadn't seen him in years, as their mothers hadn't stayed in contact.

"Rowan," said Anna. "Geez, it's been a while since I've seen you, we must have been little kids. I am not sure if you remember me, I'm Anna. My mum Kate was a friend of your mum's."

"Hi, Anna, I do remember you. It sure has been a while. Come in, Mum is out the back doing some work."

The house was still very much as Anna remembered. Slightly eclectic with artistic decorations, yet still neat and tidy. Sara was working at her laptop on a small outdoor table in the garden. She greeted Anna with a smile.

"Anna, look how much you have grown! You look so much like your mum. It is so nice of you to visit. Would you like a coffee?" Sara gave Anna a big hug.

"Thanks, a black coffee, no sugar would be nice."

Sara looked just the same as Anna remembered her; perfectly groomed blonde hair and makeup, still looking effortlessly attractive in her forties.

"So what brings you here, Anna? How are you and how have things been? I was so sorry to hear about your mum going missing. It was all over the news. I was thinking of you."

Anna just gave a small smile. She didn't know what to reply. *If Sara knew and she was thinking of me, why didn't she make contact? Is Sara being sincere? Was she going to tell me the truth if she did know anything?*

"I wanted to chat with you about Mum. I was hoping you might know something about her disappearance."

"Oh goodness, I haven't seen your mum in about ten years," answered Sara. "I wouldn't know anything about her disappearance. It's not suspicious though, is it? I read that the yacht capsized in a freak storm. I am really sorry. I wish I could give you some answers, but I don't know anything about it."

Rowan came outside with a hot coffee for Anna and gently handed it to her. As Anna thanked him, his hand brushed up against hers and she looked into his eyes and smiled, taking the coffee with both hands. Anna hadn't really noticed how handsome Rowan was before. She couldn't remember him being anywhere near as attractive as a kid as he was now. He was skinny and awkward looking back then, always riding a bike or kicking a football outside. They had hardly ever spoken to each other as kids.

"Your mum and I certainly had some adventures, Anna," continued Sara. "We travelled together before you were born. Kate was always such a free-spirited, kind soul. I hope she is at peace now, wherever she is."

After this comment, Anna felt she couldn't ask any more questions. This visit wasn't going quite as she planned. She thought she had better drink this coffee and get out of there, as Sara was making her feel slightly uncomfortable. Rowan kept looking at her and smiling. Anna wished she hadn't even come. She sipped at her coffee in awkward silence.

"Do you like photography, like your mum?" asked Sara.

"I do like photography and the arts, yes," replied Anna. "Anyway, I'd better be going, thanks for the coffee. I need to get back and study for exams. I just thought I would drop in to see if you knew anything about Mum and the incident."

"Thanks for coming Anna, it's been lovely to see you after all these years. I am sorry I couldn't help you," replied Sara.

Sara went to stand up and walk Anna out.

"No need to see me out, thanks again for the coffee."

Anna walked to the kitchen and placed her mug into the sink. Rowan followed her and walked her to the door.

"Lovely to see you, Anna," he said.

"Great to see you too, Rowan. See ya." Anna hopped into her car and waved to Rowan standing at the door. She could not get out of there quickly enough. *I can't believe I just did that*, she thought. *What a waste of time. Sara seemed a little different to how I remembered. I think I just embarrassed myself - but oh well. Now where do I go to next for answers?*

Chapter 4

Rowan

There was a gentle knock at the front door. Scruffy started barking and doing a little shuffle behind the front door, ready to pounce on whoever was behind it. The little dog barked at everyone who knocked at the front door, but his bark was always much worse than his bite. He would just sniff and lick whoever it was and wag his tail, once he knew they were accepted to enter the house. It was Scruffy's main job to alert Anna that someone was there, especially since Anna was usually in the house alone. Her dad was always working. Anna didn't answer the door to strangers, even though she was close to officially being an adult.

It is likely one of the neighbours dropping off another lasagne, she thought as she heard the gentle knock on the door once again. Anna peered through the sheer white curtain. She instantly recognised the tall, tanned figure standing behind the door. He had a towel draped over his shoulder and was casually sweeping his sun-bleached hair behind his ear. *Oh my goodness, what the hell is Rowan doing at my house? How does he know where I live?* Anna quickly checked her hair in the mirror before opening the door.

"Hey Rowan, what's up?" Anna was nervous but tried to play it cool.

"Hey, I thought you might want to join me down the beach?" he asked.

Anna felt suddenly shy. She didn't know what to reply; she had never had a guy turn up on her doorstep before, certainly not a good looking one like Rowan. She had planned on studying all afternoon, but a quick swim at the beach with him did sound tempting.

"Sounds good! Come in and I'll get changed for the beach, make yourself at home."

Scruffy shuffled around Rowan's feet, excited a visitor had come. As Rowan walked in and sat down on the rattan chair in the hallway, Scruffy jumped on his lap, wagging his tail.

"Scruffy!" yelled Anna. "Sorry Rowan, he's not usually like that. He must be excited to get a visitor - we don't get many these days, unless they are leaving something on the front porch."

"It's fine, I love dogs. We can bring him down the beach if you like," said Rowan, stroking his hand across Scruffy's back.

Anna smiled and closed the door to her room. Then she slumped down the back of the door in disbelief that a hot guy like Rowan was in her house, waiting for her to get changed to go to the beach. *He probably just feels sorry for me,* she thought. *That's why he's asking me to come for a swim. What bathers am I going to wear? Oh my, I can't believe this, my bathers aren't even in my room. I haven't even put the laundry away, they are still in the laundry.* Anna stood up and walked past Rowan.

"Sorry, just grabbing my bathers from the laundry, I won't be a sec," said Anna, smiling through her embarrassment.

"All good." Rowan smiled back.

"How did you know where I lived, by the way?" asked Anna.

"I remembered coming here with Mum when I was about five. I remembered your street led straight down to the beach and your house had the white fence with a big frangipani out the front. So I was relying on your house not changing much in thirteen years!" Rowan laughed.

"Ha! You must have a good memory; I can't even remember you coming to this place. Lucky the house hasn't changed much then, hey." Anna smiled. "If I am being honest, I had to rely on my memory to find your place also. It had been a while since I visited there with Mum."

Anna quickly retreated to her room and slipped on the pale blue bikinis her mother had bought her for her sixteenth birthday. Her thoughts wandered. *What would Mum think about me going to the beach with a guy? I mean, it's her friend's son, so I am sure she would be fine with it. I'm going to be an adult soon, so why am I even thinking about this? Mum bought me these bathers, she said they brought out the blue in my eyes. Okay Anna, get with it, come on, snap out of it and hurry up and get ready.*

Anna checked her hair in the mirror once again, quickly dabbed a tiny bit of concealer on a pimple she could see poking out of her cheek, slapped on a wipe of lip gloss, and, after sliding her feet into some thongs and grabbing a towel hanging on the back of the door, left the room.

"I'm ready, let me just get my keys." She smiled at Rowan as he stood up from the chair.

As they walked down the street together towards the shoreline, Anna felt a sense of nervousness, excitement and calm all at once. Rowan wasn't like most other nineteen-year-old guys she knew. He had a maturity about him beyond his years. Maybe it was because he had to become the man of the house at a young age, when his father left. Rowan made Anna feel relaxed, something she hadn't felt in a long time.

"So how is the search for clues about your mum's disappearance going?" asked Rowan.

"Well, it's not really. I can't help but think your mum knows more than she is telling me, but I'm not sure where to go to next or who to seek information from."

"I heard Mum talking to your dad about it on the phone, after you left our place the other day," said Rowan.

"She was talking to my dad? I didn't even know they spoke to each other. What were they saying?" Anna was intrigued.

"I don't really know - something about a medical deal that your mother knew about? It must be something to do with a company that works within the hospital, who knows," replied Rowan.

Anna felt uncomfortable and her thoughts began to race. *Why is Rowan telling me this? It is not his fault, maybe he's just being honest. What medical deal were they talking about, and what did my mother have to do with it? Why did Sara say she didn't know anything about my mother's disappearance, but then called my dad? I can't keep questioning him about it, we are supposed to be enjoying the beach. I am just going to have to reply as though I am not bothered.*

"Oh okay, interesting," she replied casually.

They arrived at the beach, and Rowan dropped his towel and thongs on the sand and jogged down to the water. Anna did the same. She noticed how captivating his smile was as he jumped into the water, and how the sun reflected off his tanned skin. Scruff followed them both into the water, wagging his tail.

As they waded in the calm ocean shallows, Rowan asked if Anna surfed. "No, I don't, maybe I will learn how to one day," she replied.

"I can teach you," he offered.

"That would be nice," Anna beamed. She couldn't believe that a guy like Rowan seemed interested in spending time with her. It felt nice. Today, for the first time in ages, Anna didn't feel so alone in the world. As they splashed around in the water, laughter echoed in the air as they gently flirted with each other. Scruffy kept swimming around them, into shore and back again.

"He's going to tire himself out pretty quickly," laughed Rowan.

"He goes everywhere I go," replied Anna. "Especially since Mum has gone, he doesn't leave my side."

"He's a cool dog. It must be hard for you without your mum, I remember you were close. I know what it's like to have only one parent. My dad left when I was young." Rowan was looking at Anna. "You have your mum's nice curly hair," he complimented.

Anna smiled, embarrassed. She wasn't used to receiving compliments; she was a loner at school and stayed away from others.

The breeze started to pick up and the waves were reaching the shore with more force. As Anna and Rowan walked out of the water together, he said, "I will grab us a coffee from the van. I remember - black, no sugar. Do you want something to eat?"

"No thanks, a coffee would be nice though. Thank you," replied Anna.

As Anna spread her towel out on the sand and lay down to soak up the warmth of the sun, she looked out at the ocean and watched the ripples of water travelling to the sand. She couldn't help but think of the words her mother had said about ripples and the truth, and felt more determined than ever to find that truth.

Rowan quickly returned with coffees in hand.

"Thank you," said Anna. She noticed the water droplets still running off Rowan's chest. He sat down on the towel next to her, shuffling in closer.

"Want a bite?" he asked, shoving a bacon and egg burger in her face. "Come on, take a bite," he begged.

Anna didn't want to seem ungrateful, so she took a small bite of the burger. This made Rowan smile.

"I hope you don't mind lots of barbeque sauce," he said.

"It's fine, I can certainly taste it," she replied, with a hand over her still-full mouth. Scruffy sat at their feet waiting for any drips to hit the sand that he could gobble up.

"So what are you studying at uni, Rowan?" asked Anna.

"Physio, but I might take a year off to travel, I'm not sure. What about you? Exams are coming up, what do you plan on studying when you graduate?" he asked.

"I'm not sure yet. I don't think I'll do that great in exams with the year I have had, and I probably won't even get into uni," Anna replied.

"Of course you will, you're smart, you will get into something," Rowan reassured Anna. "You can always change your mind down the track."

"I need to get back to do some study actually, so we should probably head back soon," Anna said.

"Yeah, cool. What subjects are you doing?"

"English Lit, Maths App, History, Art and Geography," Anna replied.

"Well, you certainly are the more worldly, arty type like your mum, hey," Rowan said, smiling. "I can help you with Maths, but that is about it. All my subjects were science based."

Anna smiled. *Did he just offer to help me with my studies?* Rowan put his arm over Anna's shoulder, hugging her towel into her as if to warm her up before they set off for the walk back home.

Anna and Rowan continued to chat about life on the walk home, with Scruffy following shortly behind. As they stomped their sandy feet walking up the driveway, Scruffy ran to the front door.

"You are not going inside with all of that sand on you Scruff, hose time first!" laughed Anna.

Scruff followed them to the hose at the side of the house. As Anna grabbed the hose to wash their feet and Scruff, Rowan gently grabbed Anna's phone out of her other hand and said, "I am going to add my number into your phone before you forget to."

Anna smiled. *Ding ding.* Rowan's phone alerted him to a message. "Geez, I better see which hot girl is sending me messages," he joked.

Anna grabbed her phone back off him, realising Rowan had sent himself a message from her phone. She looked at it. "Thanks for today, I would love to do this again. Next time, can you teach me to surf?"

The three dots started appearing already as Rowan was messaging back, "Sure, that would be great."

"I guess you are teaching me to surf then," Anna said, smiling.

As she turned the hose off and Scruffy ran around the back yard doing zoomies, Rowan hugged Anna goodbye. Feeling awkward, Anna didn't know what to do. She stayed in his embrace. As they slowly pulled away from each other, Rowan went to kiss her goodbye, but not knowing how to react, she turned her head. Rowan planted a kiss on her cheek and whispered in her ear, "I look forward to surfing with you soon."

As he walked away, Anna could not wipe the smile off her face. What had just happened?

Rowan gave a wave and a grin as he drove off. Anna looked down at her phone to look at the messages on her phone from him once again. She smiled at his cheekiness. She realised he had saved his name into her contacts as Rowan with a surfboard emoji. This made Anna smile once again.

As she went inside to study, her mind struggled to concentrate on Geography and History - she was too busy daydreaming and thinking of Rowan. Anna could not believe what happened today. For the first time in a long time she felt a glimmer of hope about the future. And for the first time in a long time, she was thinking about something other than her mother's disappearance.

Chapter 5

Stormy Weather

Strong winds were howling outside, causing the window shutters to bang loudly. As Anna walked outside to close them, Scruffy at her feet, she noticed the grey clouds that were settling in quickly from the coast. Summertime brought summer storms. It reminded Anna of the times she and her mother would race down to the beach when they saw those purple clouds coming in, to take stunning beach storm photographs. One of Kate's lightning photos over the beach had won a major photography award. The large, framed photo sat above their sofa in the lounge room. Looking at the picture made Anna reminisce about all the fond memories she had of her mother in her happy place, being creative with nature. The sounds her mother's camera would make as she took the photos, the smell of the rain hitting the hot bitumen, the purple and orange hues of the clouds, and the photography room in her art studio.

The wind continued to whirl and howl and the sky was getting darker. Anna quickly locked up all the windows and doors and made sure nothing loose was lying around before hurrying safely back inside.

Anna cuddled Scruffy on the couch with a bowl of popcorn in front of them, watching *Titanic* on the television. Anna's father Richard was away at a medical conference in Brisbane, so Anna was alone in the house.

"*Titanic* - not exactly the most appropriate choice in movies, Scruffy!" said Anna to her dog.

Ding, ding. Anna's phone echoed with a message alert. She hoped it was from Rowan. They had been messaging for weeks now and he had been teaching her to surf some mornings. Anna checked her phone straight away and read his message.

"Hey babe, is it okay if I head over to yours? I just had an argument with Mum and want to get out of here before this storm hits."

"Of course, see you soon. xx" replied Anna promptly.

I wonder what he was arguing with his mum about, thought Anna. *I thought it was only girls who argued with their mothers.*

She got up from the couch to brush her hair and check her face in the mirror. She sprayed some perfume on her neck, put some earrings on, changed her loungewear for a beach dress and applied some mascara to her lashes. She heard Rowan's car pull into the driveway. Scruffy ran to the door all excited - he already knew the sound of Rowan's car. "Geez Scruff, if your tail wagged any faster, it will fall off!"

Anna unlocked the door. The wind had increased even more and the palm trees out the front were starting to arch over.

"Quick, come inside," greeted Anna, as she let Rowan inside and locked the door behind him. He kissed her lips with relief and held her in his arms.

"What happened with your mum? Is everything okay?"

"I don't really want to talk about it," replied Rowan. "She is not the person I thought she was, let's just say that."

Anna wanted to know what the argument was about, but she wasn't going to push the issue. She could tell Rowan seemed irritated and bothered by what went on at home. He just wasn't himself.

Rowan sat down on the couch and shovelled a handful of popcorn into his mouth.

"So, what are we watching? *Titanic*? Geez, I didn't think you would want to watch a movie like this with what happened to your parents' boat and all."

"Well, there wasn't much to choose from and I am a sucker for romance movies," replied Anna.

"Is that so," said Rowan. "Maybe I need to show *you* some romance.' He leaned forward to kiss Anna softly on the lips. Then he grabbed the back of her neck and kissed her with more passion. As Rowan and Anna moved even closer on the couch and continued kissing, the television suddenly turned off, and the kitchen went dark.

"Great, the power is out," said Anna.

"Where's the torch?" asked Rowan. "My phone is nearly out of battery, so I don't want to use my phone."

"In the bottom kitchen drawer," replied Anna. The sun was setting, but there was just enough light to navigate the kitchen. Rowan found the torch and turned it on. He opened the front door, which flung open with the force of the wind, and walked to the meter box, squinting in the rain. He noticed that the streetlights were off and the neighbouring houses also seemed to have no power. Quickly heading back inside, Rowan locked the door behind him.

"Looks like the whole street is out," he said. "Maybe a tree has come down in the area."

"Great, what are we going to do now?" said Anna.

"I can think of a few things we can do," replied Rowan with a cheeky grin. Anna playfully slapped his arm as if to tell him off for his comment. Rowan pulled her towards his chest and began to softly kiss her neck, slowly moving all the way down to her belly button. Still kissing her, he slowly started unbuttoning the front of her dress.

"Is this okay?" he whispered in her ear.

Anna closed her eyes and let Rowan continue to kiss her body.

"Yes," she whispered back.

She took a deep breath, relishing the feeling of being in Rowan's arms. Anna had never felt so desired and safe. She could smell the cologne wafting off his body as he lifted his arms to take off his t-shirt. He dropped it on the floor and lifted Anna up gently, still kissing her, and carried her to her bedroom as flashes of lightning lit up the room in bursts. Scruffy followed them into the room, scared of the thunder and lightning.

"Come on Scruff, give us some privacy," joked Rowan.

Anna laughed. "He's scared, we can't kick him out of the room. He will just stay in his dog bed. Maybe we should play some music so he can't hear the thunder as much, it might help calm him."

Rowan lay next to Anna on the bed and stroked her hair. The storm outside seemed to be ramping up. Anna turned the Bluetooth speaker on and linked it to her phone to play some easy listening music.

The mellow guitar strings of the music settled the room. "See, that's better," said Anna.

"Who is this playing? Sounds like Ziggy," said Rowan.

"It is Ziggy, I love his music," Anna replied.

"Now, where were we, Miss Anna?" Rowan said, continuing to slowly unbutton the pearl shell buttons on Anna's dress while kissing her passionately. She felt his hands run over her body. Anna had never gone this far with anyone before, and she felt her nerves start to take over, and her hands trembled.

"Are you okay?" Rowan asked. "Do you want me to stop? We can stop and just cuddle if you want. I don't want you to do anything you're not comfortable with."

"It's okay," Anna replied. "I am just nervous, I haven't done anything like this before. It's not that I don't want to, I'm just feeling a little anxious, like - what if you don't like it or I don't do it right or I disappoint you."

"Anna, I am crazy about you, I want to express to you the way I feel about you by showing you, but I only want to if it is something you're okay with. I care about you, I only want to if you want to, otherwise I am happy to wait until you are ready." Rowan hugged her head into his chest.

Anna felt safe, she felt cared for and the feelings she had developed for Rowan over the last few weeks were feelings she had never felt before. Anna wanted to make love to Rowan more than anything - she just had to relax those nerves.

"Have you got protection?" she whispered, as Rowan started kissing her breasts. Rowan leaned over the side of the bed, searching for the pockets of his shorts. Anna could hear him opening a packet and getting himself ready.

Anna took a deep breath and closed her eyes. She placed her hands on Rowan's bare chest and began to kiss him again. As her dress fell to the floor, she realised Rowan was already undressed. She had never seen a man naked in the flesh before. She didn't have time to stare at his athletic body in the dim light, but she could feel every part of it. Her nerves began to settle as their naked bodies entwined with each other to the rhythm of the music, while they passionately kissed each other. Rowan held Anna tight in his arms as he thrust his hips towards hers. They both began to breathe at a faster pace while kissing, until the tension of their connection was finally released. Rowan let out a groan and rolled over to lay down.

As she lay cuddled into Rowan's arm with the sheet draped across her body, Anna took in the enormity of what had just happened. He kissed her forehead, still breathing heavily for air.

"That was unbelievable - well, it was for me, was it okay for you? Are you okay?" Rowan asked.

"I'm fine. I can't believe we just did that, it felt so good, I want more," said Anna as she kissed Rowan's chest.

He laughed, "You might just have to give me a few minutes!"

Anna giggled.

The two of them lay in each other's arms and chatted away about life as if they had been together forever. The violent winds and rain still battered against the windows.

"So I didn't want to ask again, and you don't have to tell me, but what happened with your mum tonight?" asked Anna.

Rowan sighed. "She found out we have been spending time together and she wasn't very happy."

Anna felt her heart sink. She didn't like causing trouble, and she didn't like feeling that she had done something wrong.

"She doesn't like me?" asked Anna.

"It's not that, I think she just doesn't want me getting involved with everything you have going on with your life and the connection with her and your mum and us knowing each other from kids."

"But she was a friend of my mum's, I thought she would be happy about that," Anna replied.

"I know, I don't know what her problem is. Maybe she is just jealous that I am an adult now and living my life and she is no longer controlling me and my attention."

Anna's mind started to overthink. Maybe what had just happened was a mistake. Rowan could see Anna was starting to feel anxious again.

"Hey, it's okay, I don't care what my mum thinks, I am an adult and can make my own decisions. I am glad we had the argument, as I came here and got to be with you and look what just happened!" Rowan kissed Anna on the cheek.

Anna felt a sense of contentment to be in Rowan's arms, but she couldn't shake off what he had said about his mother not wanting him to be spending time with her. As the storm outside started to abate, the television turned back on, along with the lights in the kitchen.

"Well, the power is back on now, we can watch that movie." Rowan smiled as he stood up and started getting dressed. Anna couldn't help glance at his naked body once again. Rowan didn't seem phased at all, he even lent over with everything on show and kissed Anna on the forehead as he was pulling his jocks up above his knees. Anna draped the sheets over her body and collected her dress from the floor, before stepping into it and pulling it up over her body. As they both walked into the lounge room to sit on the sofa together, Anna couldn't stop staring at the award-winning storm photo of her mother's. It had a different importance to her now. She glanced over at Rowan and smiled to herself. Those feelings she had just felt moments ago were so wonderful, she wanted to hold onto them for as long as she could.

Chapter 6

Replicas

"Anna, I'm off to work!" yelled Richard down the hallway. "I have some guests from the medical board coming over for dinner tonight, so make sure the house is clean and tidy please," he said as he closed the front door.

Anna didn't even have time to answer, he was so quick to get out the door. *I think I might have plans for tonight*, Anna thought to herself. She didn't want to be home with all the pompous laughter of the medical board and their lingo. Anna grabbed her phone and texted Rowan.

"Hey babe, do you want to head out somewhere tonight? Dad is having the medical board members over for dinner and I don't want to be around. Where shall we meet?"

Within moments, Rowan texted back.

"Sounds good. How about the Marina boardwalk at 6?"

Anna sent a love heart emoji for her approval and got up out of bed. She looked in the mirror and realised her earring had come loose from the latch and needed tightening. She knew her mum had a little jewellery tool set in her bottom drawer, so she walked to her parents' bedroom to collect it. As she bent down to pull the drawer open, she accidentally pulled the whole drawer out and it landed upside down on the floor, tipping its contents out. As Anna collected everything that fell out, she noticed a little wooden box hiding underneath the drawer. She opened it. She couldn't believe what she was looking at. Two pieces of gold jewellery that were so familiar to Anna - her mother's wedding ring and a gold bracelet. Anna's heart sank. She didn't understand - these were the two pieces of jewellery that were found after her mother disappeared. *How did they get here?* Anna held the box in her hands and raced to her bedroom, where the very same bracelet and wedding ring with engraving lay on her bedside table. Anna stood there staring in disbelief.

How could there be two sets of my mother's jewellery? What did this mean? Was this a set up and my father had placed those items on the beach?

Anna sat down on her bed. She was shocked and confused and didn't know what to do or who to ask for help. Anna grabbed her phone and called Rowan.

"Hi, I need to talk to you, I found something this morning and I don't know what it means and I don't know what to do. I feel like I can't trust my dad and I can't ask him…."

"Anna, take a breath, it's okay, what did you find?" asked Rowan.

"You know how they found my Mum's wedding ring and bracelet on the beach? Well, this morning I had to get something from mum's drawer and it fell on the floor. Underneath the drawer, there was a box and inside it was another wedding ring and bracelet, exactly the same."

"What do you mean?" asked Rowan, "Maybe they were put there when they were found?"

"No, Rowan - there are now two sets of the same pieces of jewellery, even the rings are engraved the same. The other ones are in my bedroom. This is all so suss. Maybe I need to take the jewellery to the police this morning."

Rowan paused. "Hang on, don't jump the gun and call the cops right away, maybe we investigate how this has happened ourselves. Can we confront your dad?"

"I can't tell Dad I found them, he's the one that has put them there, he's involved for sure," Anna insisted.

"Well, go and hide them in a safe place for now and we can talk about a plan to deal with this tonight," said Rowan. "It's going to be okay babe, just try and stay calm and don't overthink this. Easier said than done, I know."

"Okay, see ya tonight," Anna replied.

Anna got off the phone and started to cry. She knew this was confirmation of something suspicious going on and felt helpless. *Why would there be two sets of identical jewellery? It had to be a set up, but who was behind this, and who knows about it?*

Anna had so much study to do for her final exams, but there was no way she was going to be able to focus on learning about the history of world wars when all she could think about was the double set of her mother's jewellery she had just found. *I have to go see Aunt Jane*, Anna decided. As she grabbed the keys to her car, Scruffy ran to the door with excitement.

"All right then, you can come Scruff," Anna said to her dog, and he wagged his tail as he followed her out the door.

On the short drive to Aunt Jane's house, Anna's mind swirled. Was her mother still alive? Had her death been staged… could her own mother and father be involved in it all? As Anna pulled into the driveway, she saw Jane out the front, wearing a gardening hat and pruning the dead fronds of the palm trees. She smiled as Anna and Scruffy hopped out of the car together.

"Hello Anna, what a pleasant surprise. Having a break from the studies?"

"Something like that," Anna said.

Jane could tell Anna seemed agitated, rummaging in her handbag as she searched for something.

"What's up Anna? You don't seem yourself, how about I put the kettle on?" Aunt Jane removed her gardening glove and placed her arm around Anna's shoulder.

Scruffy raced down the hallway in the house he knew so well, looking for the children.

"They're at school Scruff, it's just me home, you scallywag," Jane said, patting him on the head.

Anna sat down at the kitchen table and opened the box, but didn't say anything.

"Your mum's jewellery - why did you bring that here?" asked Aunt Jane.

"This isn't the jewellery that was found at the beach, Aunt Jane - that is in my bedroom," said Anna. "This is a replica of the same jewellery. I accidentally found it in Mum's drawer this morning. I don't know what this means. I think I need to go to the police with it."

Aunt Jane looked at her in disbelief. "Why would your mum have a second set of the same jewellery hidden away?" she asked.

"Exactly - unless it was made before Mum went missing and she didn't even know about it. It all seems a bit suss to me."

"Have you asked your dad?" asked Aunt Jane.

"No way, he doesn't even know I've found it, and I am not going to ask him. He's the one who probably put it there."

Aunt Jane understood, agreeing with Anna with a silent nod. "Maybe best you contact the police then. I will call them now."

As Aunt Jane picked up her mobile phone to call the police, Anna stared out the window, lost in a gaze of thoughts. She could hear Aunt Jane's voice in the background, but wasn't processing what she was saying.

"Anna," said Aunt Jane, with the phone at her ear. Anna seemed to still be in her own world. "Anna, the police are going to send someone around here now to take a statement. They are probably going to want to see the other set of jewellery so we might have to duck over to yours to grab it before they arrive."

Anna just nodded. Everything was becoming too much for her. One year on from her mother's disappearance and all those feelings she put away had resurfaced again.

"There is just no closure, Aunt Jane, like I don't know who to trust, I feel like I can't even trust my own father. People are hiding the truth about what's really happened, and I need to find the truth for my own peace."

"I know darling, it's not fair. You can stay here tonight if you like," said Aunt Jane.

"I can't, I mean I have plans tonight with someone."

"Who might that be with? Do tell?" teased Aunt Jane with a smile.

Anna didn't want to say, but she didn't want to lie, either. She was dealing with uncovering lies and didn't want to create more trouble.

"I have been seeing someone, he's lovely, his name is Rowan, his mum was a friend of Mum's, but she doesn't know the extent yet, so please don't say anything, Aunt Jane."

"Rowan, Sara's son? Oh my goodness, how did this happen? When did this happen?" said Aunt Jane, sounding shocked.

"We have only been seeing each other for a couple of months, it just happened unexpectedly. I went to visit Sara to find out if she had any information about Mum's disappearance and Rowan was there. I hadn't seen him in years. He came around a week later and we started hanging out together."

"Sara doesn't know?" Aunt Jane asked.

"Well, she knows we started hanging out, and she wasn't happy about it so no, we haven't told her we are actually in a relationship," explained Anna.

"Rowan is going to tell her soon. We just thought we best wait, as she is protective of her only son."

"Your mum and Sara hadn't spoken in years, I don't really know what went on there, so maybe wait until the right time to reveal you are dating her son," agreed Jane. "Your mum would be happy for you; she always liked that kid. Show me a photo then, let's have a look at him!"

Anna had a few photos on her phone of him, as well as some of them together at the beach. She scrolled through them with her Aunt Jane.

"He's a good looker Anna, no wonder you're smitten. I'm happy for you. He looks a lot like his dad, I remember him," said Aunt Jane.

"You knew his dad? Rowan said he left when he was young."

"Yeah, we all use to hang out when we were younger, he took off when Rowan was only about five - he probably hardly remembers him. Anyway, we better dash over to your place to get that jewellery before the police arrive."

Anna couldn't help but wonder what had happened with Rowan's father. She hadn't asked

Rowan much about his father or why he had left all those years ago. She knew there had to be more to the story.

Chapter 7

Law

Bang, bang, bang! There was a stern knock on the front door.

Aunt Jane hurried to open it. Two uniformed police stood there.

"Hello, I'm Senior Detective Boyd and this is Constable Rover. We are here to look at some jewellery that might have something to do with the disappearance of Kate Mears."

"Come in," said Aunt Jane.

Anna could feel the nerves vibrate through her body as the police officers walked down the hallway. They smiled at Anna when they walked in, sitting down opposite her.

"Hello," said Anna.

"You must be Anna, Kate's daughter," said the constable. "Where is the jewellery?"

Anna handed over the jewellery on the table. The police officer started filling out a form in his folder, noting the date and time and address and details of the report.

"Where was this found, and why would you like to report this as a suspicious matter?" asked the detective.

"Well, I was looking for something in my mum's chest of drawers this morning and the bottom drawer fell out," explained Anna. "I found this wooden box underneath it, and inside was this jewellery. It is exactly the same as my mum's jewellery that was found washed up on the beach and what you have kept in evidence. It's like a replica of it."

"How do you know it's the same?"

"I know it is exactly the same, because my mum always wore them. I don't have any doubts," Anna replied confidently.

"Have you spoken to your father about this?" questioned the detective.

Anna paused. "No I haven't. I don't think I was supposed to find it, and what if he has something to do with it?"

The policeman wrote in his document folder but didn't say a word. He placed the jewellery into a bag and placed a sticker label on top.

"Right, well, we will take this evidence and be in touch if we have any further questions. We advise you to keep this conversation to yourself until we have investigated this matter further." Detective Boyd glanced over at his colleague as they both stood up ready to leave.

Anna could feel the tension but didn't know what else to say.

"Thank you for coming out. Can you please keep us posted on any updates?" asked Aunt Jane.

"We certainly will, Mrs Debrov, thank you for reporting the matter so promptly." The two men walked out the front door.

Aunt Jane closed the door and gave Anna a hug. "You did good Anna, it's going to be okay, they will investigate it and hopefully get to the bottom of things. Try not to stress about everything and let them do their job. You just enjoy your evening with the handsome Rowan." She gave Anna a wink.

"Also, your eighteenth birthday is coming up soon, are you going to have a celebration?"

Anna looked at her aunt with a serious face. "No, I don't want to do anything. Not with everything going on at the moment. I have exams, and Dad will only invite his arrogant work colleagues along and make it all about him. Plus it won't be the same without Mum there. I might just do something with Rowan - if his mum allows it, that is."

"Don't worry about her," said Jane. "Sara always likes to be in control of things, and now that her son is an adult she probably can't cope with the thought of no longer being in control of his life."

"What happened with Mum and Sara? You must know something about why they hadn't spoken in years," asked Anna.

"Well, I don't know all the details, but I think it had something to do with Sara's divorce. Since Rowan's dad left, your mum wouldn't have anything to do with her. It was probably the last time you two love birds saw each other, as young kids."

Anna got lost in her thoughts. She tried to remember the last time she had seen Rowan as a kid - it was probably when she was just starting school. She remembered her mum and Sara being close and seeing each other all the time, and Rowan riding his bike up and down the driveway while she picked flowers in the garden - yet they hardly spoke.

"I do remember this one time when the ice-cream van came down the street and we ran inside begging Mum to buy us one. She gave us the money so we could buy them ourselves, but I dropped mine walking up the driveway and started crying. Rowan offered me his just to shut me up, I think," recalled Anna.

Aunt Jane laughed. "See, he was always a kind soul, just like his dad."

"What was his dad like?" asked Anna.

"He was really lovely, actually. Handsome, kind, intelligent and very down to earth. It really surprised me when he just took off all those years ago."

"Rowan doesn't seem to have many positive things to say about his father, but he doesn't even know him, only what Sara has hold him. Apparently, they never heard from him again and he likely lives in another country."

Aunt Jane raised her eyebrows. "That is interesting. I wonder what went down for him to run away like he did. Like your mum always said: the truth will reveal itself one day. Maybe Rowan will see him again sometime, who knows. It is an absolute spin-out that you two are dating - who would have thought, hey?"

Anna smiled.

Chapter 8

Happy Birthday!

Rowan grabbed his phone from the bedside table and texted Anna. *"Happy birthday, beautiful, I can't wait to see you tonight. Xx."*

He got up and walked to the bathroom. As he washed his hands, his mother came into the bedroom.

"How is my boy? Want to head out for dinner tonight?".

"I can't," said Rowan, "I have plans for tonight. It's Anna's eighteenth birthday, so I am taking her out for dinner."

"What are you wasting your time with that troubled girl for?" Sara asked her son. "You need to focus on your studies. She has her own issues to deal with, and I don't want you getting dragged into them."

"What is your issue with her? Her mother was your best friend, for god's sake. My studies are nearly finished for the year, and you have no idea how amazing that girl is, so I am not asking for your permission or approval on my girlfriend." Rowan was angry.

"Girlfriend! Since when? Are you serious? You are calling her your girlfriend now? I just don't want you to get hurt and I am looking out for you… Rowan?"

Rowan slammed the bedroom door in her face and started to get dressed. His mother's high heels could be heard tramping back down the hallway and out the front door. As soon as Rowan heard the front door slam, he left his bedroom and headed into the kitchen. The draft from the doors slamming had blown some paperwork onto the kitchen floor. Rowan bent down and picked it up. It was a bank transaction statement for Offshore Medical Enterprises. As Rowan read the title of the document, he remembered the name being the company of Anna's father. He took a photo of the statement and had the urge to send it straight to Anna but stopped himself from pressing the send button. It was Anna's eighteenth birthday, after all.

Rowan grabbed his laptop and keys and headed out the door to uni, but he couldn't help feeling sick to the stomach about what he had just seen. Just like Anna, he knew there were secrets to be uncovered, but he didn't know where to start digging. As he hopped in the car and placed his university books on the passenger seat, he took a deep breath and sighed. He knew he wouldn't be able to face a day of lectures, so he decided to head to the shops to buy a present and card for Anna instead.

Anna was at home, coming to terms with spending her eighteenth birthday without her mum. Her dad was at work as usual and Scruffy was by her side on the couch. Anna sipped her coffee with her knees up on the sofa. She had a sadness about her today that she hadn't felt since the night her mother had disappeared. It was like the pain had resurfaced with the reality of celebrating her birthday without her mum. The minutes turned into hours and she must have fallen asleep, because she was woken by the sound of a message on her phone. *"Pick you up at 5, birthday girl xx."*

Anna jumped off the couch, not realising the time and regretful of wasting her birthday. She raced to the bathroom and into the shower. As she turned on the hot water, tears began to stream down her face. She slumped down onto the shower floor, letting the water meld with her tears. She let out all her emotions until she couldn't cry anymore. When she was spent, she got herself up, washed her hair and hopped out of the shower to get ready for dinner with Rowan. Standing in her underwear at the mirror, she dusted her face with some bronzer, mascara and lip gloss and stared into the mirror. She didn't recognise the girl in front of her. She had grown and changed so much in recent months. Anna stood staring at herself for a moment, taking in the new woman that stood before her. Then she took in a deep breath, headed to the wardrobe, and chose her outfit for the evening - a white lace beach-style dress. She took it off the hook and stepped into it, adding her pearl earrings and spraying her neck with perfume. When Scruff started wagging his tail at the front door, she knew Rowan had arrived to pick her up. He let himself in with a bunch of flowers and a small gift in his hand.

"Happy birthday beautiful, you look gorgeous!" he said, kissing Anna on the lips and giving her a hug.

"Thank you," she smiled.

"I can tell you've been crying though - are you okay?" he asked.

"Yeah, I'm fine. I've just been struggling with celebrating my birthday without Mum today. These flowers are beautiful! Can I open the gift?" Anna asked, deflecting the conversation.

"Of course!" replied Rowan, as Anna opened the small box covered in red ribbon.

"This is beautiful Rowan, you didn't have to get me this, it must have cost you a fortune! I love it!" Anna took the delicate gold necklace with a wave pendant out of the box and pulled her curly hair up so Rowan could place it around her neck. Anna kissed Rowan again to thank him for the gift.

As they left the house to head to the car, Scruffy followed.

"Sorry mate, you can't come tonight," said Rowan, picking up the dog and placing him inside the house before shutting the door.

The drive down to the restaurant was a little awkward. Rowan could tell Anna wasn't feeling in a party mood, so he held her hand with his free one and embraced the silence with a smile.

The couple talked through dinner about their studies, enjoying their meal together. Rowan was careful to not broach the topic of conversation about Anna's mother, even though he wanted to tell her about the bank statement he'd found earlier that day. The waitress brought out a small cake with candles and the restaurant started singing happy birthday. Anna's face blushed with embarrassment.

"Did you organise this?" she smiled up at Rowan.

"I may have had something to do with it," he replied, laughing.

As Anna blew out the candles, she closed her eyes and made a wish.

"What did you wish for, babe?" asked Rowan.

"Well, if I told you then the wish wouldn't come true, would it?" said Anna.

Chapter 9

Mind Games

Rowan dumped his bag at the back door and walked inside the house. He was greeted by his mother and two women Rowan had never seen before. He noticed the younger woman, a tall blonde beauty, smile at him as if she were expecting his arrival. Rowan knew his mother and the games she played and felt she was up to something.

"Rowan this is Amanda, a colleague of mine, and this is her daughter Isla; she is studying commerce at the same university you're at. It's a wonder really that you don't know her already," said Sara.

"Hello Rowan, we have heard all about you," smiled Amanda.

Rowan smiled back and raised his hand in a wave at the visitors. He noticed Isla was very easy on the eyes, and he couldn't help but hold a gaze her way. Isla in turn flicked her long blonde hair across her shoulder while maintaining eye contact with Rowan.

"Why don't you show Isla around, take her down the beach and hang out so Amanda and I can catch up on some work talk," said Sara. "They are staying for dinner, so you have plenty of time."

Rowan was already feeling uncomfortable. "I've just come from the beach. I'm going to take a shower," he replied as he walked down the hallway to the bathroom.

As Rowan closed the door of the shower, he felt the anxiety rush over him. He knew his mother was playing her usual games, but there was no point in him confronting her as she would just deny it. He was holding onto the guilt of not telling Anna about the bank statement and now his mother was presenting him with another girl of interest.

Rowan took his time in the bathroom, hoping to avoid dealing with the women in his living room. His phone beeped with a message from Anna. *"Hey babe, thinking of you. xx."* Rowan hearted the message and replied with a rushed *"Me too babe xx."*

He felt another rush of guilt. *When am I going to tell Anna about that bank statement?*

As he was getting dressed he couldn't help but overhear the topic of conversation in the living room.

"She is mentally unwell, the poor girl," Rowan heard his mother say. "She has lost her mum and dealing with a lot I know, but she's not someone I want my son involved with. I think she needs some serious help. She always was a strange character as a child, such a loner." Rowan felt angry that her mother would say such horrible things about his girlfriend. He didn't know how he was going to hide his anger, but felt he had to go along with his mother's plans so he could find out more about what was really going on.

Rowan emerged from the bedroom in his sporting attire, towel drying his wet hair. His aftershave wafted through the room.

"Nice scent," smiled Isla, looking at him. She stood up and walked over to him, starting a conversation about university. Rowan scanned the room and could see his mother and her colleague smiling at them. He turned and walked back down the hallway but Isla followed him, picking up the guitar that was leaning against the wall.

"You play?" she asked him.

"A little," he replied. "I am certainly not much of a musician, but I can play a few tunes."

"Why don't you let me be the judge of that? Play me something." Isla was insistent.

Rowan felt uncomfortable. He didn't want to be playing guitar tunes to some random girl he had just met, even if she was easy on the eye. However, he didn't want to rock the boat with his mother either, so he picked up the guitar, smiled, and started to tune the strings.

As he started playing a tune, Isla walked over to him, bent over and whispered into his ear.

"There is something so sexy about a man with a guitar."

Rowan felt even more uncomfortable and stopped playing.

"I think dinner will be ready soon," he said. Isla smiled; it was if she was happy making him feel embarrassed.

Rowan sat through dinner with a pit in his stomach. He knew his mother was scheming something, and he felt constant guilt for not telling Anna about the bank statement he'd found. And now he felt further guilt about the footsies game Isla was playing with him under the dinner table.

Chapter 10

The Kiss

Anna

Anna pulled her car up out the front of Rowan's house, Scruffy sitting in the front passenger seat wagging his tail. She had decided to pay Rowan an impromptu visit after how spoilt he made her feel on her birthday. As she turned the engine off and opened the car door to get out, she saw Rowan standing outside the front door with a tall blonde girl. Her long hair was blowing in the breeze, and her short dress revealed long, slender, tanned legs in high heels. Rowan hadn't even noticed Anna's car pull up; he seemed too engrossed in the girl standing before him. Anna felt sick to the stomach as she watched the girl lean in and kiss Rowan on the lips, holding the embrace for a few seconds. Anna stood there in shock, completely frozen. She couldn't move. A middle-aged woman quickly walked out of the house and got in her car, followed by the blonde, who gave a cheeky wave to Rowan as the car started backing down the driveway. Anna guessed it was a mother and daughter duo, but she had no idea who they were - or why one of them was kissing her boyfriend!

Anna stood motionless, not knowing what to do or say. Her trance was quickly broken by the screech of car brakes and the heart-wrenching yelping of a dog. It was only then that Anna realised Scruff had run out of the car to greet Rowan at the same time the two women in the car were rapidly reversing out of Rowan's driveway.

"Scruffy!" Anna screamed, running over to her precious pooch, who was covered in blood and whimpering in pain.

"Look what you've done!" she screamed. "My Scruff! Didn't you even look, you idiot?" Tears were rolling down Anna's face. She scooped up her beloved dog and ran to her car in desperation, holding Scruff in one arm while starting the car with the other. Scruff was limp and whining in pain. Anna didn't even have time to put her seat belt on, or notice Rowan running down the driveway to her car. He banged on the bonnet of the car shouting, "Anna, stop, let me help!"

Anna could not even look at Rowan after what she had just seen. Scruffy was her best friend, and she couldn't bear the thought of life without him as well as her mother. Every horrible thought was going through her mind, and the world around her became a blur. She raced through the streets, steering with one hand, tears rolling down her cheeks. There was a vet on the main road that Anna was praying was open. She squealed into the parking lot, and ran towards the building with the limp, bloodied dog in her arms. A gentleman holding a white cat opened the door for her.

"Help, Scruffy has been hit by a car, help me, someone help me," cried Anna to the lady at the counter.

A young vet nurse ran over and said, "Come with me," as she guided Anna and her injured dog into the emergency room. Anna placed Scruffy down on the table. His shabby fur was stained red and his body was limp. The whimpering sound he had been making had stopped.

"No! Scruffy!" cried Anna.

The vet entered the room. "Please go wait in the waiting room, we will do all we can," he said kindly.

Anna couldn't function. She was heartbroken at the thought that she might lose her loyal dog. As she walked back into the waiting room, she saw Rowan sitting on a chair.

"What the hell are you doing here?" said Anna. "Go away, I don't want you here. I can't even look at you. Why don't you go look after your new blonde girlfriend? I never should have come to your house. This would have never happened, it's all my fault for even thinking I meant something to you."

Rowan stood up and put his arm on Anna to calm her down. "Anna, you mean everything to me, I can explain, it's not what you think. That girl is nothing to me. Let's just worry about Scruffy right now."

"Get out, get away from me!" Anna screamed at Rowan. She picked up her phone, sobbing. She wanted her Aunt Jane.

People in the waiting room were all looking at Rowan and he started to feel embarrassed. He opened the door and sat down outside on the pavement with his head in his hands.

"Aunt Jane, Scruffy was hit by a car. I'm at the Northside Vet, please help me." Anna was sobbing so hard she could barely speak anymore, so she hung up the phone. The air in the waiting room was tense. The old man holding the white cat came and sat beside Anna.

"They will do everything they can, love; he's in good hands here. Do you want some water?"

Anna shook her head and sat in silence. The ticking of the clock could be heard in the waiting room, with the occasional faint sounds of barks and meows in the background. It wasn't long before Aunt Jane arrived. She hugged Anna closely and wiped her tears.

"Is that Rowan outside?" asked Aunt Jane.

"Probably, but I don't care, I don't want him anywhere near me," replied Anna.

"What happened? I thought things were going so well between you both?"

"His new girlfriend and her mother are the reason Scruffy is even here! They ran him over in Rowan's driveway. I can't even talk about it right now. All I can think of is my dog," cried Anna.

"What do you mean, his new girlfriend?" asked Aunt Jane. Anna didn't answer, she just sat in silence with tears rolling down her face.

"Okay love, I won't ask anymore now, we can talk about that later. I called your dad to let him know and he said he will get home from work as soon as he can."

The vet pushed open the double doors and pulled off his mask. Anna stood up in anticipation of the news.

"Scruffy is now stable, but he's sustained a lot of serious injuries. The next twenty-four hours are going to be critical. He's suffering internal bleeding, a broken leg, fluid on the lungs and abdominal trauma. He will need further surgery. The cost for his care with these kinds of injuries could exceed $5000."

Anna was just relieved that Scruffy was still alive.

"Thank you. The cost doesn't matter, just please save Scruffy. He's everything to me," pleaded Anna.

Aunt Jane hugged Anna just as Rowan walked back into the clinic.

"Is Scruffy going to be okay?" he asked.

"What the fuck do you care! He's fighting for his life, no thanks to you and your escapades," yelled Anna.

"Anna, it's not what you think it is!" replied Rowan.

Aunt Jane grabbed Rowan's arm gently. She could see the sadness and desperation in his face.

"Probably best you wait outside," said Aunt Jane, and walked outside with him.

"Rowan, I am Anna's Aunt Jane. I remember you from when you were young, you're Sara's daughter. Anna is in a lot of pain right now. I don't know what has gone down between you both but it's probably best you leave her alone for a little while."

Rowan put his hands in his face.

"You know my mum then, and the games she plays?" Rowan tried to explain. "This is all her fault. She invited this woman and her daughter over to try and set me up because she's not happy about me being with Anna. When they were leaving, the daughter kissed me and Anna must have seen it from her car. I didn't even know she was there. Then Scruffy ran out and got run over. This is a disaster and I can see why Anna hates me right now, but it is not how it seems."

Jane put her arm around Rowan. "Just give her some space and time. She loves that dog more than anything, and he's now fighting for his life. She misses her mum, she has just turned eighteen, she's doing exams - her world is a little crazy right now."

Rowan seemed grateful for Jane's support. "Can I give you my number then, so you can update me on how Scruffy is going? I don't think Anna will be talking to me anytime soon."

Aunt Jane pulled her phone out of her pocket. "Sure," she said, handing it to him.

"Thanks, and let me know if I can do anything to help," said Rowan, punching in his number.

"I will. Look after yourself, Rowan."

Aunt Jane walked back inside the waiting room, but Anna was no longer there. She must have gone in to see Scruffy with the vet. Aunt Jane sat down in the waiting room and took a deep breath. As she looked around a room full of people cradling their pets, she was filled with nostalgia and memories of her sister Kate. She remembered when she and Kate were young and playing cricket with the neighbours' kids. Their labrador Charlie desperately wanted to join in and got knocked out by the cricket bat. She remembered Kate picking him up and running up the hill with him to the vet. The labrador was as big as

Kate, but she carried him the whole way, determined to save her dog. Anna was just like her mother Kate; she loved dogs and would do anything for the people she loved.

Chapter 11

Mental

Anna woke to the sound of the window banging in the morning breeze. The birds in the large frangipani tree out the front were chirping away. She looked down towards the end of the bed, expecting Scruffy to be there as always. It was then that the reality of what transpired yesterday hit her like a freight train. She pushed her head into her pillow and wished it were all a bad dream. Anna placed her hands over her face and sighed. It took all her strength to get herself out of bed. She had to head to the veterinary hospital to see Scruffy as soon as she could. As she arose, her father knocked on the door and entered.

"Morning, Anna. I will take you to the veterinary clinic this morning," he said. "We will leave in fifteen minutes."

Anna looked at her dad strangely. Very rarely was he even home, let alone offer to be there for her, so she was dubious. But right now she didn't have the energy to argue or question his motives.

"Okay Dad, I'll get dressed now," she replied.

As they hopped in the car, neither of them said a word. Anna put her headphones on, so she didn't have to talk to her father. Within minutes of driving down the road, Anna noticed he had turned the car in the opposite direction of where Scruffy was fighting for his life.

"Where are you going, Dad? The vet is that way."

"Oh, I just have a few errands to do first and then we will go there," he replied, not looking at her.

Anna rolled her eyes. She should have known her father was too selfish to dedicate the morning to her and Scruffy completely. She continued scrolling through her phone with her headphones on.

After a twenty-minute drive, Anna's father pulled into a parking lot of what looked like a medical centre. Anna presumed he must be doing something for work until her dad said, "Anna, I want you to come and see someone with me."

Anna read the sign on the rendered brick wall of the building. "Healthy Minds Clinic for Adolescents".

"What the fuck, Dad?" Anna yelled.

"Anna, I have been really concerned about your mental health lately, and I think you need some help. Stalking Rowan is how Scruffy got run over in the first place."

"Stalking Rowan, what the fuck, Dad! Who told you that? Sara? I wasn't stalking Rowan! We have been in a relationship, or at least I thought we were until I saw him kissing someone else! You think I am some crazy stalker?" Anna answered angrily.

"Listen to your rage, Anna. Your grades are suffering, you're hearing voices, you are behaving erratically and you aren't coping with the death of your mother." Anna's father seemed too calm. "I really think you need to stay at this clinic for a while so you can get some help."

"How do you know she's dead? Did you kill her? You can't make me stay at a clinic! I am an adult. You can't make me do anything. I am going to see Scruffy." Anna tried desperately to leave the car, but her dad had locked the doors. Two men dressed in nursing uniforms approached her side of the car.

"What the actual fuck, Dad? You are forcing me into a mental facility because you think I am crazy?

I am not crazy, take a look in the fucking mirror!" shrieked Anna.

"Don't make this any harder than it already is, Anna, I am trying to help you. Hopefully, you can talk to someone and get some medication to help you, and your life will get better."

As Anna's dad pressed the button to unlock the car doors, Anna tried to force her way out. The two men grabbed her arms.

"Get your fucking hands off me!" yelled Anna. "You can't touch me or I will sue your ass! I am eighteen years old and I do not consent to any treatment. You would need a voluntary treatment order to do that, and Dad is not a psychiatrist! So, move before I call the police!" They loosened their grip on her arms. Anna could tell neither of them were fully aware of the situation and only following orders by some strings her father had pulled. Anna started running away.

"Anna, you are making a mistake," yelled her father after her. "This is going to help you!"

Anna was furious. She could feel the adrenaline pumping through her veins as she ran down the busy highway with her phone in her hand. She didn't even look back to see if her father and the men were chasing her, she just kept running. When she finally stopped to get her breath, she looked at her phone, wanting to call someone for help. But who? She sat down on the pavement and started to cry. *How could this be happening?* she thought. *How could they make her out to be crazy?* Anna felt so betrayed and alone. She didn't know what to do. She thought of her mother and what she would do in this situation, but that just made the tears flow even more. Anna felt that this must have been what her mother experienced being married to that man - having your feelings completely dismissed and made out to be crazy. And all while poor Scruffy was fighting for his life. It was thoughts of Scruffy that made Anna pull herself together. She knew she had to get herself to the vet as soon as possible, but she was too far from home to walk back to get her car. She impulsively decided to call Aunt Jane to come and get her. She spoke fast among the tears.

"Hello, Aunt Jane. I need you to come and get me, Dad tried putting me into a mental health clinic this morning and I've run away. I need to get to the vet to see Scruffy!"

"He *what*? Where are you?" asked Aunt Jane.

"I don't even know." Anna looked around for some signs and then down at her phone for the maps app.

"I am on the main highway… hang on, I am on Mapleton Road, near Winston Ave."

"Okay, I just need to drop the kids off at school first and then I will be there. Where is your dad?"

"I don't know, I ran away, the place was about eight hundred metres away from here. There were two guys in nursing uniforms ready to lock me up in the psychiatric hospital!" said Anna.

"Just hang tight and I will be there as soon as I can," said Aunt Jane. "I'll call you when I am nearly there."

"Thanks Aunt Jane, I don't know what I would do without you. I am going to keep walking south along the main road," said Anna.

The weather was already humid for so early in the day and there was no breeze about. Anna found a nearby tree to sit under to take a break. She sat down on the shady grass and felt all her anger turn to an overwhelming sadness. The sadness then became anxiety and overthinking. *What if Scruffy dies? What if my father did kill Mum and it was all part of his plan to make me out to be crazy? What about the jewellery replicas?*

Anna became trapped in her cycle of overthinking and couldn't escape. She had flashbacks of seeing Rowan kiss that girl and Scruffy being hit by the car. *That girl is much prettier than me*, she thought. *No wonder Rowan wants to be with her. Maybe Rowan thinks I am crazy too!* The sound of her phone ringing snapped her out of her negative thinking trance. It was Aunt Jane. "I must not be far away from you now Anna, walk to the roadside so I can see you… hang on, I can see you standing near the tree, I am pulling over now." Anna hung up the phone without speaking. Aunt Jane pulled the car over and hopped out.

"Come here, darling," said Aunt Jane, hugging her niece tightly. Anna rested her head on Jane's shoulder and cried once again.

"Let's go see Scruffy, hey," said Aunt Jane, helping Anna into the car.

"I can't go back home AJ, can I come and stay at your place?" said Anna.

"Of course hun," replied Jane, rubbing her hand on Anna's leg in a show of support.

"AJ, do you think there is any chance that Mum disappeared on purpose to get away from Dad? Like, do you think she is actually dead, or do you think she might be behind her own disappearance?" asked Anna, her face smudged face with tears.

"Well, I don't know the truth, but I do know one thing, your mum would never leave you, Anna. She loved you more than anything and she never would have left, which makes me feel if she were alive somewhere, she would definitely be here right now. I know I will never replace your mum, but I am always here for you, darling girl. You will never be alone."

Anna's eyes welled up with tears once again as she looked out the window.

"Thanks AJ."

Chapter 12

Truth

It had only been a week, but Anna was getting a little tired of sleeping on the couch at Aunt Jane's, and was sick of waking up to the sound of cartoons on the television. Anna missed her bed and her house, and being surrounded by everything that reminded her of her mum. Most of all, she missed Scruffy.

Anna glanced down at her phone. There were thirteen missed calls from her father, and four from Rowan.

"Morning! I bet you can't wait to pick up Scruff from the vet today!" said Aunt Jane.

Anna smiled, "I sure can't! I think I will drop by home to grab some more of my stuff on the way to the vet."

"Fair enough, do you want me to come with you?" asked Aunt Jane.

"No, it's fine, I'll park down the street and walk up, so I can make sure Dad isn't home."

Anna got herself ready for the day and headed home to collect more of her belongings. She parked her car in the next street and walked around to her house, checking that her father's car was not in the driveway. Within five minutes of being in her room packing things into boxes, she heard a car pull up in the driveway and the sound of two car doors closing. Anna panicked and peeked through the curtains. Her father's car was parked out the front, and Anna could hear footsteps going round into the backyard.

What the hell am I going to do? She thought. *Dad doesn't even know I am here. I will just quietly sneak out the front door.* Just as she was about to creep out, Anna heard laughter. It was a woman's laugh. The moment Anna heard the slight cackle to the laugh, she felt sick to her stomach. It brought back memories of the night Anna had dropped the glass in the kitchen after hearing that same laugh. It was at that moment Anna realised that it had been Sara all along. Everything in Anna's body began to tremble. She was so angry and hurt, she felt betrayed and foolish. *They were happy to make me out to be crazy for hearing voices,* she thought. She knew she had to get out of there as soon as possible without being seen but she couldn't get her body to move. *Come on Anna, you can do this. You need to do this for Mum, just hold it together and creep out that front door and run.*

Anna crept soundlessly to the front door, slowly and carefully opened it and tried to close it as quietly as she could. Then she ran - down the driveway and up the street as fast as she could. As soon as she got back to her car, she picked up her phone and called her aunt.

"AJ, you won't believe this! I went to the house to grab my stuff and Dad came home, and he had someone with him," she said breathlessly. "Guess who it was?" Before AJ could even answer, Anna replied with, "Sara!"

"What the hell? Did they see you?" replied Aunt Jane.

"Nope, I crept out of there. It was definitely her voice I heard in my backyard that night. They are together and behind everything; wanting me labelled as crazy so they can keep hiding their secrets! I hate them, both of them. I reckon they killed Mum."

"Does Rowan know any of this?" asked AJ.

"Who knows, I haven't spoken to him for over a week," replied Anna.

"I think you should speak with him, Anna, I don't think he has had anything to do with any of this.

He spoke to me at the vets and said his mum had invited that girl and her mother over for dinner and he had nothing to do with it. He loves you; I could tell by the look in his eyes and how devastated he was for you and Scruff."

Anna paused and stayed quiet for a moment. "I just want to focus on getting Scruffy home safe and sound today."

"Fair enough," said Aunt Jane. "I will see you this afternoon. Bye, hon."

Anna started the car for the short drive back to her aunt's place, where she was now calling home. As she arrived in the driveway, a tall middle-aged man was standing at the door waiting for someone to answer.

"Can I help you?" asked Anna.

"Hi, I am Greg Chambers," the man said. He seemed friendly. "I was looking for Jane Debrov. I believe she lives here?"

"How do you know Jane?" asked Anna. She noticed he was dressed well and his face looked familiar, even though she had never met the man before.

"Well, we were acquaintances years ago, but she contacted me out of the blue last week regarding some things from the past and I want to talk with her about them. Are you her daughter?"

"Niece," replied Anna.

"Oh my goodness, you must be Kate's daughter!"

Anna raised her eyebrows in shock.

"You knew my mum? How did you know her?" asked Anna, intrigued.

"I was married to your mum's best friend Sara, many years ago," he replied. "We used to hang out a lot. I remember when you were little. You have certainly grown up!"

Holy fuck, thought Anna. *This is Rowan's dad! What the fuck is he doing here? Rowan hasn't seen him in years. What do I do? I can't invite him in the house without anyone else here.*

As Anna panicked about what to do, Jane pulled into the driveway, home from school drop-off.

"Aunt Jane! Rowan's dad Greg is here to see you." Anna looked at Aunt Jane with dagger-like eyes.

"You know Rowan?" Greg asked Anna.

"Oh, he was my boyfriend up until last week when I caught him kissing another girl," replied Anna, not hiding her smarminess.

"Your boyfriend! Geez, this is getting worse by the minute." Greg put his hand on his head. "I think we'd better have a chat about things."

Anna didn't know what he meant. She felt offended that he seemed to think it was a bad thing that his son was her boyfriend.

"Hello. Greg. It's been a long time. Please, come in so we can talk about things," said Aunt Jane.

As the three of them walked inside the house, Anna grabbed Aunt Jane's arm and whispered into her ear. "You contacted him, what the actual fuck? Why?"

"I felt I had to Anna, there are so many things that just didn't add up here," she replied.

"So how come you left Rowan without a dad all of those years?" Anna asked Greg, defiantly. Aunt Jane glared at her for being so rude and direct.

"I didn't leave him without a dad. Sara confessed to me that Rowan wasn't my child, that he was in fact Richard's, so my whole world came crashing down and I was left with no choice but to escape," replied Greg sadly.

Anna felt like she was going to throw up. Her knees dropped to the floor. "Rowan is my half-brother? I have slept with my brother? I have fallen in love with my brother? Does Rowan know the truth? Does my dad know?" She started to cry. Then Aunt Jane started to cry. Greg stood there awkwardly, not knowing what to do or say.

Anna continued to cry out in despair, asking all the questions she wanted answers to. "They killed my mother for sure, they wanted her out of the picture. Did my mum know what was going on? How could they be so evil? How long have they been having an affair?"

"I don't know, all I know is Sara told me Rowan wasn't mine, that he was Richard's, that they had been having an affair for years. I ran away and never looked back. I have had no contact with anyone from here for many years now, I wanted to forget about that part of my life. I was ashamed. I wanted to move forward with my life."

Anna's anger was overwhelming. "What a fucking bitch! No wonder she didn't want me dating her son!"

"I am so sorry this has happened," said Greg.

Aunt Jane gave him a hug. "None of this is your fault Greg, I knew there had to be more to the story. For you to vanish like you did all those years ago, it was obviously something big that we never knew about. This is why, with everything that has happened, I contacted you."

Anna was shaking. "Who is going to tell Rowan? He needs to know the truth!"

Anna looked more closely at Greg. She could tell he was a kind man, with good morals. She noticed Rowan had the same dimple in his chin as Greg, and the rounded shape of his ear lobes were identical, as was their side profile. The more Anna looked at Greg's face, the more of Rowan she saw.

"Did you get a paternity test?" she asked Greg. "Rowan looks like you."

"No, I didn't," replied Greg. "I left as soon as I found out Sara had been having an affair, and being told Rowan wasn't mine. I was heartbroken. I loved that boy. I couldn't deal with it."

"What if he *is* your son? What if Sara just wanted you out of the picture, like she wanted my mum gone?" asked Anna.

Greg looked down at his hands and sighed, "I don't know, I haven't thought about that. I have a wife and two daughters of my own now in Sydney, I haven't wanted to think about that time of my life, I have kind of erased it all. I haven't told them about my past, I am so ashamed."

Anna was sitting crossed legged on the floor, and Aunt Jane was leaning on the kitchen bench with her head in her hands. Greg was standing behind the couch. All three of them held a silence that seemed to go for eternity.

"What are we going to do?" asked Anna. "Do we call the police? I know they have killed Mum, but what evidence and accusations do we have about these evil people, other than they've fucked up our lives!"

"I think we need to talk with Rowan, get a paternity test done and go from there. I think until we know more, we keep this conversation to ourselves," said Greg.

Aunt Jane nodded. "I think that's a wise plan. I'll invite Rowan here to see Anna and make sure you are here so he can hear it from you, Greg. How about meeting here tomorrow morning around ten? We need to go and get Anna's dog Scruffy from the vet now."

Greg gave the thumbs up. "I will see myself out. See you both tomorrow."

Anna sat on the floor in silence, still in shock and trying to digest everything that was revealed today.

Poor Rowan, she thought. *He is going to be sad, angry and hurt. How could his own mother lie to him all of these years? Well, I suppose my father has done the same to me.*

"I am in love with him, AJ, but I could be in love with my own brother," said Anna. "It makes me feel sick. How did this happen?"

"Let's just wait and see what the truth is Anna, there is no point getting yourself upset until we know the full truth. Even then we can't change things. So just be kind to yourself. Let's focus on the positives for today and go get Scruff!"

Chapter 13

Paternity

Anna was so glad to have Scruffy back in her arms. He had a bandage all the way up one leg and lots of stitches across his abdomen, but it didn't stop his tail from wagging. Anna cuddled into him and closed her eyes, whispering to her dog, "It's going to be okay bud, we are going to be okay."

There was a knock at the front door. Scruffy jumped out of Anna's arms and hobbled to the door on three legs, still wagging his tail. Anna felt the nerves rush over her as she followed Scruffy to the front door. She peered through the blinds and saw Greg standing on the other side. She opened the door and smiled, "Hi Greg, come in."

"Hello Anna, Rowan here yet?"

"No, not yet. Aunt Jane arranged for him to come over, so he should be here soon."

"I'll admit I'm bloody nervous!" Greg said with a half-smile.

"Yeah, me too," said Anna. "I haven't spoken to Rowan since I saw him kissing that girl over a week ago. Then Scruffy got hit by her car, and now this!"

"You have had a tough time lately, hey, especially with your mum going missing," said Greg. "Life can be really unfair at times. But you are young and strong, and I am sure you will get through all of this, whatever the future holds."

"Thanks, yeah it has been tough for all of us," Anna replied. "My Aunt Jane has been amazing, so I am grateful."

Aunt Jane made her way down the hallway and greeted Greg, just in time for there to be another knock at the door. This time it was Rowan.

"I think you should answer it Anna, we will wait out the back," said Aunt Jane.

Anna took a deep breath and opened the door. As soon as she saw Rowan's handsome face, the tears began to well in her eyes.

"Can I give you a hug?" he asked. "I have missed you." Scruffy was very excited to see him, standing on three legs, wagging his tail and letting out a little bark to greet him. "Oh Scruff! You are home! That is so awesome."

Rowan hugged Anna tightly and kissed her on the cheek. Anna just smiled. She didn't know what to say in the awkward situation. Aunt Jane walked back down the hallway.

"Hello Rowan, nice to see you again. There is someone else here to see you that I know you haven't seen in a very long time."

Rowan walked with her down the hallway and out the back door. When he saw Greg, he stood still. The cheery expression on his face quickly changed to serious.

"Hello, son," said Greg nervously. "I can't believe how much you have grown up." His croaky throat was choking back tears.

"What are you doing here? Why are you here? Why now after all this time?" said Rowan, confused.

Anna held Rowan's hand as he looked around the room, wondering what the hell was going on.

"Look son, firstly I want to say I am sorry. I know it doesn't mean much after all the years that I haven't been there for you, but I want to tell you my side of the story."

Anna could tell Rowan was becoming angry and agitated.

"You are not my father, what kind of father disappears and never wants to see his son again?"

"That is the thing son, I want to explain about how I ended up here. Anna's Aunt Jane contacted me last week concerned about some things your mother is up to. I haven't been back to this part of the world in over fourteen years, and I want you to know why."

Rowan had his hands in his pockets and was scuffing his feet on the ground while shaking his head in disbelief.

"Hang on, please hear me out," pleaded Greg. "Fourteen years ago, I skipped town because your mother told me you were not my child, that you were Richard's, and that she had been having an affair with him for years. I was heartbroken, so I did the cowardly thing and ran away and never came back."

Rowan looked up at him in disbelief. He could see Aunt Jane standing behind him holding her face in her hands. He turned to Anna with a face full of tears.

"You're my fucking sister!" he yelled. "Did you know this? Did any of you know this?" Rowan became angry and started walking around the backyard with his hands on his head. "This can't be happening!"

Anna walked over to him and tried to hug him.

"Rowan, I only found out yesterday and I was just as shocked as you. But then I couldn't stop looking at your dad and how much you look like him. I think you both need to do a paternity test to find out the real truth. I think your mother wanted your dad out of the picture, as well as my mum. I think both your mum and my dad have something to do with the disappearance of Mum. Sara was at my house with Dad the other day, they didn't know I was there."

"This is too much, I can't even think right now." Rowan paused. "There is something I haven't told you. On your birthday, I found a bank statement for your dad's business, Offshore Medical Enterprises, that Mum had. I wanted to tell you but didn't want to ruin your birthday." Rowan shook his head. "What a lying secretive bitch she is."

Anna hugged Rowan, resting her head on his chest. They both began to cry. Greg walked over to them both. "I think we need to get a paternity test done as soon as possible and then go and see the police with the evidence we have," he said. "If your mother has lied about Richard being your father to get me out of your life, then she's robbed me of a relationship with my son. Knowing this, I can't help but feel both Sara and Richard have something to do with Kate's disappearance. Neither of them can be trusted."

Rowan placed his hands over his face. "I can't go home tonight and face that woman."

"You are welcome to stay here, Rowan," said Aunt Jane.

"You are also welcome to stay with me at my hotel," Greg said to Rowan. "Then we can get a paternity test done first thing in the morning."

Rowan hardly knew the man, but he couldn't face going home. He nodded at Greg.

As Rowan and Greg got themselves ready to leave, Anna and Rowan hugged each other again. It was the strangest feeling for them both. They wanted nothing more than to be in each other's arms, but they also didn't feel comfortable doing so.

"I would kiss you goodbye if I was certain we aren't now related," said Rowan.

Anna couldn't help but smile. If she didn't, she would only cry again.

115

Chapter 14

Karma

The afternoon sun was glistening on the water at Sunrise Beach. Anna was sitting on her towel watching the small waves crash onto the sand. It made her think of her mother, and her theory about the ripples of water always reaching the shore, just like the truth. As Anna looked out at the surfers sitting on their boards waiting for a break, she noticed the way the waves would build momentum and then slowly fade away. Anna knew the news she was about to receive would change her life forever.

"Hello, Anna," said Greg, approaching her on the shoreline. Rowan was standing next to him and gave her a modest wave.

"This envelope is about to reveal the future, so are you ready to discover the truth together?" Greg asked.

Anna smiled.

Greg opened the envelope with his tanned hands as Anna and Rowan looked at each other in anticipation. Greg read the letter out loud.

"The DNA specimens submitted for analysis by Mr Greg Chambers and Mr Rowan Chambers determine shared genetic markers making the probability of paternity 99.99%."

Anna began to cry. Rowan grabbed her face with both hands and kissed her on the lips. Greg hugged them both with open arms. The smiles on their faces could be felt by everyone at the beach.

Greg hugged his son, "I am so sorry I haven't been here for you, Rowan. I love you and I am deeply sorry for not being the father I should have been to you. You have two beautiful sisters I want you to meet one day, and I hope we can repair all those years lost."

Rowan wiped his eyes with his sleeve, embarrassed that he had become so emotional. Anna took a deep breath and sighed. She looked out to the ocean and spoke softly to herself as the waves pulled at her toes.

Rowan put his arm around her and kissed her cheek. "Let's go straight to the police with all the evidence we have." He pulled the bank statement out of his pocket and gave it to his dad to hold, along with the paternity test results. The three of them walked to the car together as a team, headed for the police station.

When they arrived, Greg took the lead at providing their evidence while Anna and Rowan stayed quiet. After several long hours of questioning, Greg suggested they have lunch at his hotel before he flew out to Sydney that evening.

"So, will you follow in your mum's creative footsteps, Anna?" asked Greg.

"I am not too sure, I am thinking about it. I don't really know what I want to do next year."

"Well, if you have half the creative talent your mum had, then it's worth a shot. Her photography is amazing," said Greg.

As they were eating lunch, Anna received a call from Aunt Jane. She put her phone on speaker so the three of them could hear.

"Hello, Anna, you won't believe this. The police have just called to let me know that your father and Sara have been arrested and charged for the murder of your mum, as well as theft and fraud of over four million dollars. They have both been taken into custody without bail and all their bank accounts have been frozen."

"Holy shit!" said Rowan.

Anna was silent. She was relieved that finally there were some answers, but a feeling of panic rushed over her in the new reality that she was now going to be without a mother or a father. Greg put his arm around her. "Everything is going to be okay Anna, you will be just fine."

Rowan rubbed her back and kissed her on the side of the head. "We have each other Anna, it is going to be okay."

As the three of them drove home after lunch, Anna looked out of the window at the blue skies and moving clouds. She contemplated the year that had passed. *What a year it has been,* she thought. *Never could I have predicted what has transpired.*

Greg pulled into Aunt Jane's driveway and said goodbye to Anna and Rowan. They all hugged each other in the driveway, feeling a mixture of justice and sadness.

"If there is one silver lining that has come out of all of this mess, it's that I have my precious son back," said Greg.

Rowan tapped his father on the back and smiled.

"See you soon, Dad."

After Greg had driven off, Anna and Rowan were greeted by a hobbling Scruffy at the front door, which lifted their mood.

"Do you want to head home to my place with Scruff and spend the night together?" asked Anna, holding Rowan's hand.

"I couldn't think of anything I would rather do, babe," replied Rowan, as he kissed her on the lips.

That night, Rowan and Anna retired to bed after a long day they will never forget. The bedroom was filled with a warm glow from the salt lamp on the bedside table. They lay on the bed together in each other's arms, holding on tightly, not wanting to let go.

"I am so glad you aren't my sister," said Rowan, kissing Anna and running his fingers through her hair.

"Me too!" said Anna.

Rowan slowly began to unbutton Anna's pyjamas while kissing her neck. He gently made his way down her body and back to her supple lips.

"I love you, Anna," he whispered in her ear.

Anna looked into his mesmerising eyes and whispered back, "I love you too, Rowan."

Rowan pulled his shirt off and grabbed Anna's waist, pulling her closer. He ran his fingers up her thighs and started kissing her breasts. The sound of their breathing became faster and louder as they tousled under the sheets together, making love as if they had been longing for each other's body forever. All the tension of the previous days was released with their intense emotions. The sound of pleasurable groans eventually turned to silence, as Rowan kissed the tears on Anna's cheek and held her close. The lovers fell asleep in each other's arms.

Anna woke up and checked her phone. It was only five am but she couldn't fall back asleep. She turned over and admired the outline of Rowan's handsome face in the moonlight. She leant forward and kissed his sleeping forehead. Anna thought about everything she had been through. All of the heartache and pain she had endured and how much she missed her beautiful mum. *If I head down to the beach now, I will make the sunrise,* she thought. She crept out of bed quietly so she wouldn't wake Rowan or Scruff, and grabbed her mother's camera, which had been sitting on her dressing table untouched for over a year. Soundlessly, she left the house in bare feet and pyjamas and walked down to the beach. The moon glistening over the water guided her way. With the cool sand between her toes, she walked along the beach to the favourite spot where she and her mother would take photos at sunrise. As she patiently waited for the sun to finally start peeking over the horizon so she could take her photos, she whispered to the breeze blowing across the water.

"The ripples have finally reached the shore, Mum, and the truth has revealed itself. I am still waiting for more of them to reach the shore; but I am ready for whenever they arrive and I know regardless of their truth, I am going to be okay. Love you forever Mum."

Lisa Van Der Wielen is a Primary School Teacher and Author from Perth, Western Australia. Her passions for teaching and writing led her to become a Children's Author in 2017. Her books support the charities Perth Children's Hospital Foundation, Ronald McDonald House and Heart Kids Australia. Her love for the beach, nature, and dogs, provide her with inspiration to write poetry and stories that inspire.

lisavanderwielen.com

Follow Lisa on Amazon and social media using the links from her website!